The Thistle Queen

Catherine J Rosser

Published by Catherine J Rosser, 2024.

This is a work of fiction. Similarities to real people, places, or events are entirely coincidental.

THE THISTLE QUEEN

First edition. October 18, 2024.

ISBN: 979-8227606822

Written by Catherine J Rosser.

Table of Contents

Act One:
Into the Thorns

The kingdom of Farrovale lay in the grip of an unnatural blight. Crops wilted overnight, their leaves blackening as if touched by frost, and the air hung heavy with a sickly, sweet scent that lingered long after the sun dipped below the horizon. The people whispered of curses, of dark magic seeping from the ancient forest of Thrysseldown. But no one dared to venture near its shadowed borders, where the trees seemed to move with a life of their own and the thorns grew thicker than spears.

Elowen, the royal gardener of Farrovale, had noticed the creeping rot in her plants weeks before anyone else. She had spent her life nurturing the gardens of the castle, coaxing life from the soil with a skill that many considered uncanny. Her hands were roughened by work, but her eyes were keen, and she saw things others overlooked. As the blight spread, she worked tirelessly, applying remedies, potions, and charms, but to no avail. The garden continued to die, its flowers curling into brittle husks.

The rumors began as whispers among the castle servants, but it wasn't long before they reached the ears of those in power. Some claimed Elowen was a witch, that her unnatural affinity for plants had turned against them all. Others insisted she was the only one capable of breaking the curse. But as the crops failed, and the people grew hungry and desperate, fear and suspicion took hold.

One evening, as Elowen worked alone in the royal garden, she heard the guards approaching. Their torches flickered in the twilight, casting long shadows that danced like specters on the stone walls. She knew what was coming; the looks, the muttered accusations, the way people avoided her gaze. She had heard it all before—witch, curse-bringer, dark-hearted.

When the captain of the guard stepped forward, a grim look on his face, she dropped her trowel and raised her hands, showing them empty. "I've done nothing wrong," she said, but the words felt hollow.

The guards surrounded her, hands on their swords. "The crops are failing, the people are starving," the captain said. "And you, Elowen, with your strange knowledge and witch's tricks, are the only one with your hands deep in the soil."

She knew there would be no reasoning with them. The fear in their eyes was as thick as the vines that choked the distant forest. She took a deep breath, her mind racing. If she stayed, they would likely imprison her—or worse. She needed to run. But before she could act, a new voice cut through the night air.

"Well, now, that's hardly fair, is it?" a man said, stepping into the torchlight with a grin that was all charm and no sincerity. "Accusing the one person trying to fix the problem?"

Elowen recognized him instantly—Rook, the thief she had caught stealing herbs from the garden not two days before. A rogue with a silver tongue and a knack for appearing exactly where he wasn't wanted. He winked at her, a glint of mischief in his eyes.

"What are you doing here?" she hissed.

"Saving you, apparently," he whispered back, his grin never faltering. Then, louder, he said, "I think it's time we make our exit, don't you?"

Before the guards could react, Rook tossed a small vial to the ground. It shattered, and a cloud of smoke erupted, filling the air with a blinding mist. Elowen felt a hand grab hers, and she was pulled through the confusion, her heart pounding as they fled into the night.

Flight Through the City

They darted through the narrow alleys of Farrovale, the shouts of the guards echoing in the distance. Elowen's heart raced, but she matched Rook's pace, her feet sure on the cobbled streets she knew so well. As they ran, she wondered why he had saved her. What did he gain by risking his neck for hers? She would find out soon enough.

They reached the outskirts of the city, where the lights faded and the shadows of the forest loomed ahead. Rook finally slowed, leading her behind a crumbling stone wall. They crouched there, catching their breath as the guards' voices faded into the distance.

"What was that?" she demanded, pulling her hand away from his. "Why help me?"

He shrugged, his grin infuriatingly nonchalant. "Let's just say I have a fondness for lost causes. And besides, I couldn't let the only gardener in the kingdom who knows her way around deadly nightshade get carted off, now could I?"

Elowen frowned, still suspicious. "What do you want, Rook?"

"Honestly?" he said, leaning back against the wall. "I heard about the curse. Figured you'd be the one most likely to know something useful about breaking it. And if there's one thing I've learned, it's that there's profit in helping people who have a knack for growing things—especially when those things are in short supply."

"Profit." She scoffed, shaking her head. "Of course."

But as much as she distrusted him, she had no other options. The guards would be searching the city by now, and she couldn't risk returning. With a resigned sigh, she nodded. "Fine. But if you try to double-cross me, I'll turn you into compost."

Rook's grin widened. "Fair enough."

Into Thrysseldown

As dawn broke, they made their way toward the edge of the forest. The border of Thrysseldown was marked by a wall of thorns so thick and tangled that it seemed impossible to pass through. Elowen hesitated, feeling the weight of its darkness press against her senses. The forest called to her, a whispering voice in the back of her mind, but it was not a gentle call—it was a warning.

"Are you sure about this?" Rook asked, glancing at her. For the first time, his voice held a note of seriousness.

Elowen swallowed hard, her eyes fixed on the twisted brambles. "No. But if this curse really is coming from the forest, then that's where we'll find our answers."

As they stepped closer, a rustling sound caught their attention. From the shadows of the forest emerged a fox, its fur a sleek, smoky gray. It stared at them with unnervingly intelligent eyes.

"Well, well," the fox said, its voice smooth and aloof. "What do we have here? Two mortals foolish enough to venture into the Thistle Queen's domain."

Elowen jumped back, eyes wide. "A talking fox?"

The fox bowed its head, the gesture oddly regal. "Periwinkle, at your service. Or not. Depends on your intentions."

Rook raised an eyebrow. "A talking fox named Periwinkle. That's a bit precious, isn't it?"

"Blame my mother," Periwinkle replied dryly. "But let's focus on the matter at hand. You're about to walk into a place where even the shadows have teeth. And I don't mean that as a metaphor."

Elowen crossed her arms. "And why should we trust you?"

The fox's eyes glinted. "Because I know these woods better than anyone. I was once a prince, you see. A fae prince, cursed by the very queen who rules these thorns. I can guide you—if you're willing to listen."

Rook looked skeptical, but Elowen, sensing a strange familiarity in the fox's gaze, nodded. "We need a guide. And it seems you need allies."

"Wise words," Periwinkle said with a flick of his tail. "But know this: the Thistle Queen's curse is no simple matter. She is bound to the forest, and it to her. To break the curse, you will need more than bravery."

"What, then?" Elowen asked.

The fox's eyes darkened, and he whispered, "You'll need to face the thorns within your own hearts."

The Briar Court

Periwinkle led them through the forest, their path winding and twisting as if the woods themselves were alive. The further they went, the thicker the shadows grew, and the air took on a heavy, oppressive quality. Thorny vines coiled around tree trunks, and the flowers they passed seemed to turn their heads, watching with unblinking eyes.

Their first true test came when they stumbled upon the Briar Court—a gathering of fae twisted by the Thistle Queen's magic. They appeared human at first, their laughter echoing like bells, but as they emerged from the shadows, their true forms became visible. Their skin was bark-like, eyes glowing a sickly green, and their hands ended in clawed, vine-covered fingers.

Elowen and Rook were surrounded, and the Briar Court invited them to play a game—a deadly riddle challenge where wrong answers would turn them into living statues of thorns. Elowen's knowledge of plants and her quick wit allowed them to solve the riddles, but not without a price. One of the fae lashed out, scratching Rook's arm, leaving a mark that pulsed with dark magic.

As they escaped the Briar Court, Rook's humor started to falter, the mark spreading like roots under his skin. Periwinkle's warnings became more urgent, and Elowen realized they were not just fighting the forest—they were fighting themselves, and the curse that sought to claim them.

With every step deeper into Thrysseldown, the forest tightened its grip, and the whispers of the Thistle Queen grew louder.

The Deeper Paths of Thrysseldown

The forest of Thrysseldown was an ever-changing labyrinth, its paths twisting and doubling back as if guided by an unseen hand. The deeper Elowen, Rook, and Periwinkle ventured, the more the forest seemed to press in around them, its trees growing taller, their branches reaching like skeletal fingers. The air grew colder, heavy with the scent of damp earth and decaying leaves. As they walked, the shadows lengthened, and strange noises echoed—rustlings that sounded like whispers, and low, mournful cries that sent shivers down their spines.

A Game of Shadows

After their narrow escape from the Briar Court, Elowen and Rook trudged forward, their nerves frayed and their senses on high alert. Rook's arm throbbed where the fae had scratched him, the mark slowly spreading like ink beneath his skin. Despite his bravado, his face was pale, and his usual confident grin had faded.

"We should rest," Periwinkle advised, his eyes flicking warily around. "The forest has ways of wearing down those who try to brave it. It will twist the path beneath your feet, muddle your mind, and whisper lies. Best to conserve your strength."

Elowen nodded, though she felt uneasy about stopping. "How long until we reach the Thistle Queen's domain?"

Periwinkle's ears twitched. "That depends. The forest bends and twists, and the closer you get to her, the more reality will warp around you. We may be closer than it seems—or farther than you can imagine."

They set up camp beneath a large oak tree, its roots forming a natural barrier against the thorns creeping along the forest floor. Elowen gathered herbs from her satchel, carefully preparing a poultice for Rook's wound. She worked silently, her hands moving with practiced precision, though her thoughts were racing. Every step they took seemed to lead them deeper into a nightmare, and the weight of the forest's magic pressed heavily on her senses.

As she applied the poultice, Rook winced but forced a grin. "Well, I'd say that was close. Those fae weren't exactly what I'd call hospitable."

Elowen didn't smile. "You're lucky it's just a scratch. The magic in this place is... powerful. If that wound gets worse, we'll have to find something stronger to counteract it."

"Good thing we have the best gardener in the kingdom, then," Rook replied, his tone light but his eyes betraying the fear creeping in.

Periwinkle, who had been keeping watch, suddenly stiffened. His fur bristled, and his eyes glowed faintly in the dim light. "We have company," he whispered.

From the shadows beyond their camp, figures began to emerge—ghostly and indistinct. At first, they seemed like mere silhouettes, but as they approached, Elowen's heart sank. They were reflections—copies of herself, Rook, and even Periwinkle, their faces twisted into mocking sneers.

"These are shadow-doubles," Periwinkle hissed. "The forest's way of testing us. They'll show you your darkest fears, your worst selves."

The doubles circled them, their movements graceful and slow. Elowen's doppelgänger stepped forward, her face a cruel mask of indifference. "You failed them all, you know," it said, its voice a distorted echo. "Your plants, your kingdom, your family. You're just a gardener—what can you possibly do against the Thistle Queen?"

Elowen's fists clenched, but she forced herself to remain calm. "I know what I am," she said. "And I know what I can do." She held her ground, meeting the double's gaze.

Rook's shadow stepped forward next, its eyes gleaming with malice. "You think you're a hero, but you're just a coward," it sneered. "Running from every fight, talking your way out of every danger. But there are some things you can't run from."

Rook's jaw tightened, and his hand instinctively moved to the wound on his arm. "I'm no hero," he muttered, almost to himself. "But I've made it this far, haven't I?"

As the doubles circled, Periwinkle's shadow form approached him, whispering in a language Elowen couldn't understand. The fox's ears flattened, and his eyes narrowed, but he did not speak. Instead, he lashed out with his paw, and the shadow dissipated like smoke.

"These illusions are designed to unsettle us," Periwinkle said, his voice tense. "Do not listen to them. The forest wants us to doubt, to fear, to break apart."

Elowen and Rook exchanged glances, nodding as they steeled themselves. Together, they faced the shadows, refusing to be cowed. The illusions flickered, their forms wavering as if sensing their resistance. One by one, the shadows faded, leaving only the darkness of the forest.

But even as they vanished, Elowen felt the weight of their words lingering. She pushed the doubts aside—there would be time for fears later. For now, they needed to keep moving.

The Forget-Me-Knot Field

The next day, they continued their journey, following Periwinkle's lead as he weaved through the forest's twisting paths. As they walked, Elowen noticed a change in the air—a faint, sweet fragrance that reminded her of spring flowers. But something about it felt wrong, too sweet and too alluring.

"We're nearing the Forget-Me-Knot Field," Periwinkle warned, his tail flicking nervously. "These flowers are no ordinary blooms. They sing to travelers, lulling them into a sleep from which they never wake."

Rook raised an eyebrow. "Sleepy flowers? Sounds almost pleasant, compared to everything else we've faced."

"Don't underestimate them," Periwinkle snapped. "The Queen's magic runs through them. They feed off the life force of anyone who succumbs to their song."

Elowen frowned. "How do we get past them?"

"Simple," Periwinkle said, his voice laced with sarcasm. "You hold your breath, cover your ears, and hope for the best."

As they approached, the flowers came into view. The field stretched out like a carpet of blue, the blossoms nodding gently in the breeze. Their petals glowed faintly, casting an eerie light. Elowen felt a pull, as if invisible threads were tugging at her, urging her to step into the field.

"Stay close," she whispered, covering her ears as best she could.

The flowers began to hum, a soft, melodic sound that vibrated through the air. Even with her ears covered, Elowen could feel the music's pull. Her eyelids grew heavy, her steps slower. Rook stumbled beside her, his hands pressed tight against his ears, his expression strained.

Periwinkle, in his fox form, darted ahead, his fur bristling as he leapt between patches of flowers, guiding them forward. "Keep moving!" he barked. "The moment you stop, they'll take you!"

As they reached the center of the field, Elowen's foot caught on a vine. She stumbled, her hand brushing one of the flowers. Immediately, the petals curled around her fingers, and she felt a surge of drowsiness wash over her. Memories began to play before her eyes—visions of the garden she'd nurtured, the life she'd left behind. She heard her mother's voice, warm and comforting, calling her name.

"Elowen, come home."

The pull was almost unbearable. She wanted to give in, to sink into the softness of those memories, to forget the fear and the darkness. But then she heard another voice, faint and distant.

"Elowen! Wake up!"

Rook's voice broke through the haze. She blinked, the flowers' grip loosening as she pulled herself free. She reached for Rook, who was teetering on the edge of sleep, his eyes half-closed. "Stay with me!" she shouted, pulling him forward.

Together, they pushed through the last stretch of the field, the flowers' song fading as they stumbled onto solid ground. Periwinkle was waiting for them, his eyes narrowed with concern. "You're lucky," he said. "Another minute, and you'd have become part of the forest's collection."

Elowen glanced back at the field, the blue blossoms swaying gently. She felt a shiver run down her spine. "The

Queen's magic is powerful. If this is just a taste, what will we face when we reach her?"

"Worse," Periwinkle replied grimly. "The forest is her domain, and she'll use everything in it to break you."

The Hollow Man

As they pressed on, the landscape began to change. The trees grew closer together, their branches entwined like the fingers of skeletal hands. The air felt heavy, and the path beneath their feet became uneven, tangled with roots and brambles.

It was then they encountered the Hollow Man.

He emerged from the shadows, a tall figure draped in tattered robes that hung like the remnants of autumn leaves. His face was a hollow mask of straw and burlap, with two empty eyes that glowed faintly from within. His fingers, long and clawed, scraped the earth as he moved.

"Turn back," he whispered, his voice a rasping echo. "This path is not for the living."

Elowen stepped forward, her heart pounding but her resolve firm. "We seek the Thistle Queen. We will not turn back."

The Hollow Man tilted his head, as if considering her words. "To seek her is to seek your end. I guard the way—those who pass must answer my riddle, or their life becomes the forest's."

Rook exchanged a wary glance with Elowen. "We've come this far. What's the riddle?"

The Hollow Man's eyes flickered. "What cannot be seen, yet binds the living? What has no weight, yet crushes the soul?"

Elowen's mind raced, the forest's oppressive energy pressing down on her thoughts. She felt the answer on the edge of her consciousness, like a word just out of reach.

"It's fear," she said finally, her voice steady. "Fear binds us, even when we cannot see it."

The Hollow Man's eyes dimmed. "Correct," he whispered, his body slowly dissolving into the mist. "But remember—facing your fear is not the same as defeating it."

As he vanished, the path ahead cleared, revealing a trail leading deeper into the heart of the forest. Elowen, Rook, and Periwinkle pressed on, the Queen's whispers growing louder, the shadows growing deeper, as they neared the heart of Thrysseldown.

The Heart of the Forest

The path that opened before them was narrower and darker than any they had traversed. It wound like a serpent, coiling between ancient trees whose trunks were covered in claw-like thorns. The ground was uneven, filled with twisting roots that seemed to pulse, as if the forest itself were alive and breathing. The deeper they went, the more the air felt heavy, laced with a palpable sense of dread.

The whispers grew louder—faint at first, like the rustle of leaves, but soon they became distinguishable words, each one tugging at Elowen's mind. They spoke of failures, of past mistakes, of betrayals she had long since buried. She felt the pull of their truths, but she shook her head, pushing the thoughts aside.

Beside her, Rook stumbled, clutching his arm where the cursed mark had spread further. Dark veins webbed up his skin, reaching toward his shoulder. His face was pale, and sweat beaded on his brow, but he forced a smile. "Lovely place for a stroll, isn't it?"

Elowen shot him a worried glance. "The mark is getting worse."

Rook shrugged, though his expression was strained. "Just a scratch. I'll manage."

Periwinkle padded ahead, his ears flicking as he scanned their surroundings. "We're nearing the Hollow Glade," he murmured. "It's the border between the outer forest and the true heart of Thrysseldown—where the Thistle Queen's power is strongest. If we cross it, there's no turning back."

"What happens if we don't?" Rook asked.

Periwinkle's eyes glinted with a hint of fear. "The forest doesn't like intruders. If you hesitate, the path will close behind us, trapping us in the outer circle—a maze with no exit."

Elowen's gaze hardened. "Then we keep moving."

The Hollow Glade

The trio emerged into a vast clearing, the Hollow Glade, where the forest opened up like the maw of a great beast. The trees formed a perfect circle, their branches arching overhead to create a canopy of twisted limbs and thorns. The ground was littered with fallen leaves that crunched underfoot, and in the center of the glade stood a massive oak, its bark blackened and twisted into the shape of a face. Its eyes, carved deep into the wood, seemed to watch them as they entered.

"This place is old magic," Periwinkle whispered. "The heart of Thrysseldown beats from this very spot. The Queen's power is rooted here."

As they stepped further into the clearing, the whispers became a roar, a cacophony of voices that pulled at their minds. Elowen felt herself falter, the weight of the forest's magic pressing down on her like a heavy shroud. She glanced at Rook, who seemed to sway on his feet, his eyes unfocused.

"Elowen..." he murmured, his voice distant. "It feels like... like everything is pulling me under."

She reached out to steady him, but the moment their hands touched, a jolt of energy surged between them. The ground beneath them rippled, and the faces on the trees twisted, their mouths opening in silent screams. The air thickened, and a low growl emanated from the oak at the center of the glade.

Periwinkle's fur bristled. "The Queen knows we're here. We need to move—now!"

But as they turned to leave the glade, the paths they had entered through vanished, the trees shifting and closing like a trap. The branches above twisted tighter, blocking out the light, and the oak's eyes flared with an eerie green glow.

"We're trapped," Rook said, his voice tinged with panic.

Elowen took a deep breath, forcing herself to think. "No. There's always a way out. We just have to find it."

The Thistle Maze

As if in response, the ground beneath their feet shuddered, and the leaves lifted, swirling into the air. The clearing transformed into a maze of thorns and brambles that rose from the earth, creating walls that stretched high above their heads. The vines pulsed, alive with dark energy, and the air was thick with the scent of decay and sweet flowers—a mixture that made Elowen's head spin.

Periwinkle's ears flattened, and he growled low in his throat. "The Thistle Maze. It's a trial—a test of courage and will. Only those who are pure of heart or strong enough to face their fears can navigate it."

Rook forced a grin, though his eyes betrayed his worry. "Well, here's hoping we're at least one of those things."

The maze was alive, shifting and twisting as they moved. Each turn seemed to lead them deeper into its tangled depths. Elowen felt the thorns brush against her arms, and each touch left a burning sensation. The whispers grew louder, echoing in her ears with every step.

"You'll fail. You're not enough. You'll lose everyone you care about."

Elowen gritted her teeth, refusing to give in to the voices. "Ignore them," she whispered. "They're just trying to make us doubt ourselves."

But the maze had other tricks. As they moved forward, they came upon a crossroads where the paths split into three, each one disappearing into the darkness beyond. Carved into the bark of a nearby tree was a message:

"Three paths lie before you—only one leads to salvation. Choose wisely, or the thorns will claim you."

Rook scanned the paths, his hand hovering over the hilt of his dagger. "How do we know which one is the right choice?"

Periwinkle's tail twitched. "This is a riddle—a test of instinct. The Queen's magic will try to confuse you, but the answer lies in the nature of the maze itself."

Elowen thought back to everything she knew about plants and thorns. The forest was alive, but it was also rooted in deception. "The Queen's power is to manipulate and confuse," she said. "She wants us to take the wrong path."

Rook nodded. "So, we pick the one that seems the least likely?"

Elowen hesitated, then pointed to the middle path, which was narrow and overgrown, almost invisible compared to the others. "This one. It's hidden—if she wants to mislead us, the right way would be the one she hides."

They moved cautiously down the narrow path, and as they walked, the air grew colder. The whispers faded, replaced by a soft, eerie silence that was somehow worse. Elowen kept her hand on the hilt of her small knife, ready for any threat.

The Glass Pool

After what felt like hours navigating the twisting path, they emerged into a clearing where a small pool of water shimmered under the moonlight. The surface was perfectly still, reflecting the canopy above like a mirror. In the center of the pool was a single thistle flower, its purple bloom glowing softly.

Periwinkle's eyes narrowed. "The Glass Pool. It's a trap, but also a key."

Elowen crouched by the edge, studying the water's surface. She could feel the pull of magic, like a current beneath the stillness. "What do we need to do?"

Rook's eyes darted to the reflection. "It shows what you most want, but also what you fear. You have to confront it—face the truth, or the water will pull you in."

Elowen looked into the pool, and her reflection wavered, shifting until she saw an image of her garden in Farrovale, lush and full of life. But the image changed—her garden withered, the flowers turned black, and the vines twisted into monstrous shapes that lashed out, tearing apart everything she had worked to build.

The water rippled, and she saw herself—older, alone, wandering the ruins of the castle as the forest consumed it. "It's not real," she whispered, trying to tear her gaze away.

But the water pulled harder, and she felt the vines wrap around her wrists, dragging her closer. "You can't escape your fate," the pool whispered. "You will be alone, and everything you love will turn to dust."

Elowen felt the thorns bite into her skin, but she fought back, gripping her knife tightly. "No," she said, her voice firm. "I refuse to accept that."

She plunged her knife into the water, and the image shattered like glass, the ripples spreading out and breaking the illusion. The thorns retreated, and the pool calmed. The path beyond the pool revealed itself, a tunnel of vines leading further into the depths of the forest.

Rook stepped up, his eyes clouded as he stared into the pool. "It's showing me..." he whispered, but before he could speak further, Periwinkle nudged him with his paw. "There's no time. You've seen enough."

Reluctantly, Rook tore his gaze away, and together, they crossed the threshold into the next part of the maze. As they left the Glass Pool behind, the forest grew darker, the whispers growing louder and more insistent.

Approaching the Queen's Domain

As they moved further, the forest's magic began to warp reality around them. The trees twisted into unnatural shapes, their branches curling into claw-like fingers that reached for them. The ground beneath their feet seemed to pulse, and the shadows moved independently, slithering like serpents.

Elowen's senses tingled with every step, her instincts warning her of the danger ahead. She felt the air grow thick with magic, and the shadows whispered promises of power and escape, each one more tempting than the last.

"We're close now," Periwinkle said, his voice a low growl. "The Queen's domain lies ahead. Beyond this path is her court—the heart of the curse."

Rook, his hand still pressed against his wound, managed a weak grin. "Let's hope she's not expecting us."

Elowen's eyes were fixed ahead, her determination steeling her. "Even if she is, we'll be ready."

As they stepped beyond the final arch of thorns, the air changed—a chill swept through, and the darkness around them grew deeper, as if they had crossed a threshold into another world. The Thistle Queen's domain awaited, and the true test of their courage, resolve, and unity lay ahead.

The Thistle Queen's Domain

As Elowen, Rook, and Periwinkle crossed the threshold, the forest's transformation became undeniable. What had been a tangled maze of vines and brambles gave way to a vast, eerie woodland that felt both expansive and suffocating. The air hummed with energy, thick with the scent of damp earth, crushed thistles, and something metallic, like the tang of blood. The shadows grew longer, stretching unnaturally, and the trees seemed to whisper, their leaves rustling with secrets meant to ensnare.

The path was lined with flowers unlike any Elowen had seen before—petals like black silk, their centers glowing with a faint, unnatural light. They swayed gently, even though there was no breeze, and as they walked, Elowen could feel their eyes on her. She knew, instinctively, that these flowers were not ordinary; they were watchers, tendrils of the Thistle Queen's magic.

"Keep moving," Periwinkle warned, his voice barely above a whisper. "The Queen's eyes are everywhere here."

Rook glanced uneasily at the flowers. "Creepy little things, aren't they? I feel like they're whispering."

"They are," Periwinkle replied grimly. "They speak in a language you cannot hear, but they report everything back to her. We're already in her sight."

The Court of Thorns

The path led to an open glade shrouded in mist, and at its center rose a twisted structure—part palace, part organic monstrosity. The Court of Thorns stood like a monument to the forest's curse, its spires woven from thick, thorny vines that glowed faintly in the dim light. The walls pulsed as if alive, and the flowers that grew from its surface wept black sap.

Periwinkle stopped at the edge of the glade, his fur bristling. "This is it. The Thistle Queen's court."

Elowen's heart pounded. "What do we do?"

"Once you enter, the forest's magic will test you. The Queen feeds on fear, despair, and doubt—she will try to twist your minds and turn you against each other. Stay close, and whatever you see, remember that it's an illusion."

Rook rubbed his shoulder where the dark veins from the cursed wound had spread. "Easier said than done."

Together, they crossed the glade and approached the entrance of the court. The massive thorny doors opened of their own accord, groaning as if reluctant to allow them entry. Inside, the air was cold and heavy, and a soft, mournful melody echoed through the hall. The walls seemed to shift and sway, the vines curling like fingers reaching out to touch them.

As they moved further in, the interior expanded, revealing a vast hall lit by floating orbs that glowed with a sickly green light. Shadows danced along the walls, creating the illusion of faces—some screaming, others laughing, all twisted in expressions of torment. Elowen felt a chill run down her spine, but she pressed on, her hand gripping the knife at her belt.

Rook's steps slowed as the wound on his arm pulsed with every heartbeat. "Something's wrong," he muttered, his voice strained. "The walls... they're moving."

The vines on the walls seemed to pulse with each of his breaths, reaching toward him. Elowen grabbed his arm, her eyes narrowing. "Hold on. Don't let the illusion take hold."

But even as she spoke, the hall began to shift. The shadows elongated, and the walls pulled back, revealing countless corridors that spiraled off into darkness. Each one beckoned with whispers, promising escape, safety, or answers to secrets long buried.

The Hall of Mirrors

Periwinkle's eyes flashed. "This is one of her traps—the Hall of Mirrors. It shows you the path you want to take, but none of them lead to freedom."

Elowen felt a pull toward one of the corridors where she saw a vision of her garden, restored and vibrant. She could almost smell the sweet perfume of the flowers, feel the soft earth beneath her fingers. Her heart ached with longing, but she knew better than to trust it. "It's a trick," she said, pulling herself back. "We stay together."

But Rook was already moving, his eyes locked on a corridor where a figure waited—a woman with long, dark hair and eyes like emeralds. "Mother?" he whispered, his voice breaking.

The figure smiled, holding out her arms. "Rook, my brave boy, you've come back to me."

Rook's expression softened, and he took a step toward the vision. Elowen grabbed his arm, her grip firm. "Rook, no. It's not real. It's the Queen's magic."

He hesitated, torn between the longing in his eyes and the reality Elowen's voice anchored him to. The figure's smile faltered, and her eyes darkened, shifting from a warm green to an empty black. "You're always running, Rook. You'll never find what you're looking for. You'll always be alone."

The vines along the walls surged forward, wrapping around his legs. Elowen pulled harder, and Periwinkle leapt to his side, biting through the thorns with his sharp teeth. Together, they yanked Rook back just as the corridor vanished, the illusion collapsing into shadows and smoke.

Rook stumbled, clutching his arm. "I thought—" he started, but the words caught in his throat.

Elowen's eyes were soft, but her voice was firm. "That's what she wants—to make us doubt. We can't afford that."

Periwinkle nodded. "Stay focused. The Queen knows your weaknesses. She will use them against you."

The Chamber of Lost Things

The trio continued deeper into the court, the hallways twisting and changing until they found themselves before a pair of massive, iron doors covered in thorny inscriptions. Elowen pushed the door open, and they entered a vast chamber filled with artifacts—mirrors, trinkets, portraits, and objects of all kinds, each one resting on a pedestal or suspended in the air.

Periwinkle's eyes widened. "The Chamber of Lost Things. Every item here represents a soul claimed by the Thistle Queen—a life she has taken, a hope she has crushed. Tread carefully."

As they moved through the room, the items seemed to whisper, calling out to them in voices both familiar and foreign. Elowen stopped before a pedestal holding a small locket. The chain was gold, but the locket itself was covered in a tangle of thorns. She reached out, and as her fingers brushed it, a vision flashed before her eyes—a memory she had long buried.

She saw herself as a child, wandering the gardens of her home. Her mother knelt beside her, planting flowers together, their hands stained with soil. "These are forget-me-nots, Elowen," her mother had said, smiling. "They remind us of those we love."

But the vision shifted—she was older now, standing alone in the garden as it wilted, the flowers blackened and dying under a gray sky. Her mother's voice echoed, distorted and cold. "You failed me, Elowen. You couldn't save us."

Elowen pulled her hand back, her breath catching in her throat. The locket's whispers continued, but she forced herself to turn away, knowing it was another trick.

Rook, meanwhile, had stopped before a mirror. His reflection stared back at him, but it wasn't quite right—his eyes were dull, and his face was lined with shadows. "This place..." he muttered. "It's all the things we've lost, isn't it?"

Periwinkle padded closer. "And all the things we fear to lose. This chamber is designed to make you linger, to trap you in your regrets. You must resist."

As they moved deeper into the chamber, the objects grew more twisted—portraits with eyes that bled black tears, clocks that ticked backwards, and toys that whispered eerie lullabies. The room seemed endless, each step taking them further from the entrance.

But then, at the far end of the chamber, they saw it: a throne made of vines and bones, its surface polished like obsidian. Seated upon it was a figure draped in shadows, her face obscured by a veil of thorn-covered flowers.

The Thistle Queen Revealed

The figure rose slowly, her movements graceful and haunting. As she stepped forward, the veil parted, revealing a face both beautiful and terrible. Her eyes were a brilliant green, like deep forest pools, but they were cold, devoid of warmth. Her lips curved into a smile that sent a chill through Elowen's spine.

"Welcome, travelers," the Thistle Queen said, her voice like the rustling of leaves in a storm. "You've come far, but this is where your journey ends."

Elowen stepped forward, her hand gripping the knife at her belt. "We've come to break the curse."

The Queen laughed softly, the sound echoing through the chamber. "Oh, brave words, little gardener. But do you know the price of breaking a curse as old and deep as this one?"

Rook's hand tightened on his wound, the veins pulsing under his skin. "We'll do whatever it takes."

The Queen's eyes flicked to Rook, and she smiled, her gaze like a serpent's. "Even if it means losing what little remains of your life?"

Elowen felt the weight of her words and the power behind them. She knew this was the moment that mattered most—the point where the truth of the curse would begin to unfold. "We're not afraid of you," she said, though her voice trembled slightly.

The Queen's smile faded, and her eyes darkened. "Oh, you should be. For I am not merely the ruler of this forest—I am its heart. And unless you are prepared to face the thorns within your own souls, you will never escape."

With a wave of her hand, the chamber shifted, the walls dissolving into a storm of thorns and shadows. The ground split beneath them, and the darkness reached up like grasping hands. The Queen's voice became a whisper in the wind, a promise and a threat.

"Let the trials begin."

And with that, Elowen, Rook, and Periwinkle were plunged into the heart of the Thistle Queen's power, their greatest fears coming to life as they faced the trials that would determine whether they would break the curse—or become its next victims.

Trials of the Thistle Queen

Elowen, Rook, and Periwinkle stood in the midst of swirling shadows, the walls of the chamber dissolving around them like smoke. The air was alive with the scent of earth and flowers, but also a metallic tang—blood and fear, mingling as the forest's magic grew thicker. The Queen's laughter echoed in the distance, a sound both melodic and menacing.

"Face your truths," her voice whispered, disembodied and distant. "Only those who survive their darkest fears may hope to break the curse."

The ground beneath their feet shuddered, and they found themselves standing at the edge of a vast abyss. The floor was fractured, and beyond the cracks lay nothing but darkness. Slowly, the world around them shifted, the fragments of the chamber pulling apart and reassembling into three distinct paths, each leading into a separate, shadowy expanse.

Periwinkle's eyes narrowed. "The Queen is separating us."

Rook's face paled. "Why? We need to stay together."

"It's part of the test," Periwinkle replied, his voice grim. "The Queen knows that united, we're stronger. She wants to isolate us, to turn us against ourselves. Each of us must face our own trial."

Elowen took a deep breath, steeling herself. "We've come this far. We can't turn back now."

The trio exchanged determined glances, each knowing they had no choice but to confront what lay ahead. As they stepped toward the paths, the shadows twisted, pulling them apart. The darkness rose like a wall between them, and for a moment,

Elowen felt the weight of isolation press upon her. She shouted for Rook, for Periwinkle, but her voice was swallowed by the abyss. The air grew colder, and the path before her seemed to stretch on endlessly.

Elowen's Trial: The Garden of Loss

Elowen walked forward, her hand gripping the hilt of her knife as she entered a new, unfamiliar landscape. The air felt different here—thin, tinged with a sense of sadness that settled in her chest. Before her stretched a garden, but not one filled with the vibrant life she loved. This garden was a decaying wasteland, the soil cracked and barren. The flowers were wilted, their petals black and brittle, and the trees stood like skeletal remains.

At the center of the garden, she saw a single figure kneeling in the dirt, tending to a patch of withered forget-me-nots. Elowen's breath caught in her throat. She knew this figure.

"Mother?"

The woman looked up, her face worn and lined with sorrow. "Elowen, my dear," she said, her voice soft but laced with pain. "Why did you let it all die?"

Elowen's heart ached, and she took a hesitant step forward. "This isn't real. You're... you're gone."

But the vision of her mother persisted, her eyes full of disappointment. "You were supposed to protect the garden, Elowen. It was your gift. Your calling." The woman gestured to the ruined landscape around them. "And yet, everything withers under your touch."

The ground trembled beneath Elowen's feet, and she felt the vines wrap around her ankles, pulling her down. "I tried," she whispered, her voice cracking. "I tried to save it."

Her mother's expression hardened. "You failed. And now, you're alone."

Elowen felt the vines tighten, the thorns digging into her skin. The weight of her past mistakes, of every plant she couldn't save, every life she couldn't protect, pressed down on her. The whispers grew louder, merging into a single, condemning chorus: "Failure. Failure."

She closed her eyes, the pressure building, threatening to crush her spirit. But then, a small voice inside her pushed back—a spark of defiance. "No," she whispered. "I am not defined by my failures."

She reached into her satchel, pulling out a small pouch of seeds she always carried. With shaking hands, she scattered them across the dead soil. "I will not let this be the end. I still have the power to bring life."

The vines recoiled as the seeds began to sprout. Green tendrils emerged from the cracks, and flowers bloomed—bright blue forget-me-nots that glowed with a soft, magical light. The garden slowly came back to life, color returning to the landscape as Elowen's resolve grew stronger.

The vision of her mother faded, her face softening into a smile. "You are stronger than you know, Elowen."

The path beyond the garden opened, and Elowen stepped forward, feeling the weight lift from her shoulders. She knew her trial was only beginning, but she felt a renewed sense of purpose.

Rook's Trial: The Hall of Echoes

Rook found himself alone in a vast, echoing chamber filled with mirrors—each one reflecting not just his image, but his past. The walls were lined with portraits of his many faces—laughing, sneering, crying, all versions of himself he'd hidden behind.

As he moved through the hall, the mirrors shifted, and he saw memories he'd long tried to forget. He saw himself as a child, hungry and cold, stealing bread from a market stall. He saw himself older, conning nobles and commoners alike, his charm a mask for his fear. And then he saw his mother—her face pale, her eyes filled with a pain he'd never been able to ease.

"You always run, Rook," a voice echoed from the mirrors. "You always run and leave everyone behind."

He stopped before a mirror that showed him standing alone, the world around him crumbling. "I don't have a choice," he said, his voice trembling. "I do what I have to."

The mirror's surface rippled, and the image changed. His mother appeared, her expression full of sorrow. "You left me, Rook. You let the world break you."

"No," he whispered, his hand pressed against the glass. "I tried. I couldn't—"

The glass cracked, and the figure of his mother reached out, her hand cold against his. "You've always been afraid of standing still, of facing the truth."

The chamber darkened, and the mirrors shattered, the shards spinning around him like a storm of broken memories.

Each one whispered his failures, his regrets, his fears. The darkness pressed in, threatening to consume him.

But then he remembered Elowen's face—her determination, her strength. She had believed in him, and that belief gave him strength. "I'm not running this time," he said, his voice stronger. "I've found something worth standing for."

He reached out, and the shards coalesced into a single mirror, showing his reflection not as a broken man, but as someone whole—someone capable of change. The storm quieted, and the path forward opened.

He stepped through, his grip tightening on his dagger. He had faced the truth of his past, and though it still hurt, he knew he was ready for whatever lay ahead.

Periiwinkle's Trial: The Circle of Regret

Periwinkle, separated from his companions, found himself in a circle of standing stones, each one carved with runes that glowed a deep blue. The air was thick with magic, and he felt the weight of his past settle over him. The forest around him was silent, but the stones whispered secrets—secrets he'd hidden even from himself.

A figure appeared—a fae with golden eyes and a crown of thorns. His own reflection, the prince he had once been.

"You failed them," the reflection said, its voice cold. "You failed the Queen, and you failed yourself."

Periwinkle's fur bristled. "I did what I had to. I was betrayed."

The reflection's eyes flashed. "You betrayed her first. You were supposed to protect the forest, to guard the realm. Instead, you let love blind you, and now you're cursed—nothing more than a fox playing at being a prince."

The stones pulsed with light, and images of his past flashed before him—his life at the Queen's side, the love they shared, the moment he turned away, and the curse that followed. Each vision was a reminder of his choices, of the life he'd lost.

"I know my sins," Periwinkle growled, his tail flicking. "But I'm here to set things right."

The reflection's expression softened. "Are you truly here to break the curse, or to reclaim the power you lost?"

Periwinkle hesitated, the weight of the question pressing on him. He had lived so long in this form, hiding behind bitterness and sarcasm, afraid to confront his true intentions. But now, faced with the chance to undo his mistakes, he knew the answer.

"I'm here for them," he said, thinking of Elowen and Rook. "And for her."

The reflection nodded, the stones dimming. "Then prove it."

The path opened, and Periwinkle moved forward, his eyes fixed on the distant light. He had faced his past, and he would see the curse broken—even if it meant sacrificing the last remnants of his former self.

Reunion at the Edge of Darkness

The paths converged, and Elowen, Rook, and Periwinkle found themselves back in the heart of the Thistle Queen's domain. They had faced their trials, each emerging with a renewed sense of purpose.

The Queen awaited them, her eyes cold and calculating. "You have survived my trials," she said, her voice a mix of curiosity and anger. "But the final test remains."

Elowen stepped forward, her eyes blazing. "We're ready."

The Queen's smile was a blade, sharp and mocking. "We shall see." She raised her hand, and the forest around them roared to life, the thorns rising like a wave to engulf them.

The final battle for Thrysseldown had begun.

The Final Test

The forest roared to life, and the ground beneath Elowen, Rook, and Periwinkle shuddered as the thorns surged, twisting into a living wall of jagged vines and razor-sharp leaves. The Thistle Queen's eyes glowed with a fierce, unnatural light as she stood at the center of the storm, her power radiating outward. Shadows danced at her feet, swirling around her like a living cloak.

"Do you really think you can break my curse?" she taunted, her voice echoing through the clearing. "This forest has taken hundreds before you. It feeds on fear, and you are nothing but prey."

Elowen felt the thorns pull at her feet, tightening their grip as they tried to drag her down into the earth. She gripped her knife tightly, slashing at the vines, but they seemed endless, growing faster than she could cut them away. "We won't be prey," she shouted, her eyes locked on the Queen. "We came to end this."

Rook and Periwinkle flanked her, their eyes sharp and determined. Rook, despite the curse spreading up his arm, wielded his dagger with precision, cutting through the vines that reached for him. Periwinkle, now a blur of fur and sharp teeth, tore through the brambles, his growls echoing through the clearing.

But the forest was relentless. The vines hissed and snapped, moving like serpents as they coiled around their legs and arms, seeking to immobilize them. The Queen raised her hands, and the shadows at her feet elongated, forming figures—warriors made of pure darkness, their eyes burning with a sickly green fire.

The Battle in the Glade

The shadow warriors charged, their movements swift and silent. Elowen blocked the first blow with her knife, the impact sending a shock up her arm. She gritted her teeth, pushing back as she felt the power of the forest coursing through her opponent. The shadows were solid, tangible, and they fought with a fury she hadn't expected.

Rook danced around his opponent, using his agility to evade their strikes. Despite the wound on his arm slowing him, he fought with a newfound determination, his blade flashing as he deflected each attack. "These things don't go down easy!" he called out, dodging a strike aimed at his chest.

Periwinkle leapt from shadow to shadow, his fox form quick and agile. His teeth tore through the dark figures, but each time one fell, another seemed to rise in its place. "We can't keep this up forever!" he growled, his fur bristling.

Elowen realized they were being overwhelmed. The Queen's magic was too strong here, and the forest itself was fighting against them. They needed to shift the balance. "We have to draw her out," she said, slashing through another vine. "We need to make her come to us."

Rook nodded, parrying another blow. "And how do we do that?"

Elowen's eyes scanned the battlefield, her mind racing. The Queen's power was tied to the forest, but she was also the heart of it. "We need to disrupt her connection to the forest. If we weaken the bond, she'll be forced to engage directly."

She reached into her satchel and pulled out a vial of oil infused with herbs and seeds—an old remedy she'd crafted to encourage life in struggling soil. "This will counteract her magic, but we need to get it to the roots."

Periwinkle's eyes flashed. "The roots are beneath the court. We'll have to break through the thorns."

The Queen's laughter echoed again, and the shadow warriors pressed closer. "Your efforts are futile," she hissed. "This forest is my domain."

Elowen took a deep breath, steeling herself. "Rook, cover me. Periwinkle, help me get to the roots."

Together, they pushed forward, fighting through the thorns and shadows. Elowen and Periwinkle carved a path through the forest floor, tearing away the layers of vines. Rook held the shadows at bay, his dagger moving like lightning as he blocked and parried their attacks.

The thorns clawed at Elowen's arms, but she pressed on, digging through the tangled roots. She could feel the magic pulsing beneath the soil, dark and twisted. As they broke through, she poured the oil into the earth, whispering a chant under her breath—a prayer to life, to light, to break the darkness.

The Queen's Fury

The moment the oil touched the roots, the forest recoiled. The ground shuddered, and the shadows wavered, their forms flickering. The Queen's expression twisted into a snarl as she felt the disruption. "You dare defy me?" she roared, her voice a mixture of rage and pain. "You will suffer for this!"

Elowen, Rook, and Periwinkle regrouped as the Queen stepped forward, her eyes blazing with fury. She raised her hands, and the forest itself seemed to scream. The thorns pulled back, and the ground opened, revealing a chasm of swirling darkness. From the depths emerged monstrous forms—creatures made of thorns and bone, their eyes burning with the same green fire as the Queen's.

"We need to stop her now!" Rook shouted, his voice strained as he fought back another wave of shadows. "She's throwing everything at us!"

Elowen's heart pounded as she faced the monstrous creatures. The Queen was drawing on the full power of the forest, and the energy in the air crackled like a storm about to break. She could feel the pulse of magic beneath her feet, the heartbeat of the forest fighting against her.

But then she saw it—a weakness in the Queen's defense. As the Queen channeled her power, her focus was split, and the shadows that surrounded her wavered. "Rook, Periwinkle—we need to strike together, all at once."

Periwinkle's eyes met hers, and he nodded. "Aim for her center. That's where her power is most concentrated."

Rook, despite his exhaustion, grinned. "I've always wanted to take down a queen."

The Confrontation

Elowen gripped her knife, feeling the magic surge through her veins. This was the moment. She knew that the Queen's power was immense, but it was tied to the forest—if they could sever her connection, they could weaken her hold.

As the three charged, the Queen raised her hands, and the air around them crackled with dark energy. Lightning-like tendrils of magic shot out, aiming to strike them down, but they moved as one—Rook deflecting the blows with his dagger, Periwinkle darting forward, and Elowen pressing the attack.

The Queen's eyes narrowed, and she focused her power, sending a wave of force that knocked Rook back. He hit the ground hard, the impact forcing the air from his lungs, but he struggled back to his feet, his determination unwavering. "Keep going!" he shouted.

Periwinkle leapt at the Queen, his form shifting in mid-air. For a brief moment, Elowen saw not a fox, but a fae warrior with eyes like gold. Periwinkle struck at the Queen's shield of shadows, his claws tearing through the dark magic.

"Now!" he cried.

Elowen lunged, her knife aimed for the Queen's center. As she made contact, she felt the resistance of powerful magic pushing back, but she pushed forward, channeling everything she had into the strike. The knife pierced the Queen's shield, and there was a moment of stillness—a heartbeat where the air itself seemed to hold its breath.

Then the world exploded into light.

The force of the impact sent Elowen flying, the power of the Queen's magic blasting outward like a shockwave. She landed hard, the wind knocked out of her. For a moment, all she could hear was the roar of the forest, the screams of the shadows, and the crackle of energy as the Queen's power fought against the disruption.

When the dust settled, Elowen struggled to her feet, her vision blurred. The Queen was on her knees, her face contorted with rage and pain. The connection between her and the forest was broken, and the shadows that had protected her flickered, their forms collapsing into nothingness.

Rook staggered to his feet, clutching his side, while Periwinkle stood, his fur matted but his eyes glowing with determination. "We've weakened her," he said, his voice steady. "But the final blow must come from you, Elowen."

Elowen took a deep breath, feeling the magic still thrumming through the air. She approached the Queen, her knife raised. "This ends now."

The Queen looked up, her eyes burning with defiance. "You think you've won? The forest and I are one. Destroy me, and you destroy everything."

Elowen hesitated, the weight of the decision bearing down on her. She knew the forest was tied to the Queen's life, but she also knew it didn't have to be that way. The forest had once thrived without her curse, and it could again. "It doesn't have to be like this. You don't have to be the forest's prisoner."

The Queen's eyes softened for a brief moment, a flicker of pain crossing her face. "It's too late for that."

Elowen stepped closer, her voice firm. "It's not. Let me free you."

She reached out, not with her knife, but with her hand, placing it over the Queen's. The magic pulsed between them, and Elowen felt the weight of centuries—the pain, the grief, and the loneliness that had bound the Thistle Queen to this place. She channeled her own magic, the life-giving power she had nurtured her entire life, into the Queen's heart.

There was a moment of silence, and then a surge of energy flowed through the clearing. The thorns receded, the shadows faded, and the forest seemed to sigh, releasing a breath it had held for ages.

The Queen's form began to change. The thorns fell away, and the shadows lifted, revealing a woman with silver hair and eyes like deep forest pools, filled with both sorrow and relief. She smiled, her face softening. "Thank you, Elowen."

As the last of the shadows faded, the Queen dissolved into light, her form scattering into the wind like petals. The forest around them began to bloom, the thorns replaced by flowers of every color, the trees bursting with life.

Elowen, Rook, and Periwinkle stood together, watching as the forest came alive. The curse had been lifted, and the Thistle Queen's power was gone, leaving behind only the promise of renewal.

But their journey was not yet over. As the forest transformed, a path opened—a path that led to the heart of Thrysseldown, where the true secret of the forest, and the Queen's curse, waited to be revealed.

Act Two: The Heart of Thrysseldown

The air in the transformed forest was alive with new energy. The heavy, oppressive aura that had once suffocated every breath was replaced by the scent of blooming flowers and the sound of rustling leaves. Light filtered through the canopy, creating a patchwork of shadows and sunlit paths. But despite the transformation, Elowen, Rook, and Periwinkle knew their journey was far from complete.

As they stood together, catching their breath, Periwinkle's eyes fixed on the newly revealed path that led deeper into the forest. It was lined with flowers that seemed to glow with their own light, petals in shades of blue and silver. The air was charged with magic, ancient and powerful.

"That path..." Rook began, his voice uncertain. "Where does it lead?"

Periwinkle, still in his fox form, tilted his head. "To the heart of Thrysseldown—the true source of the Queen's power. The curse may be lifted, but the magic that sustained it is still there. If we don't face it, the forest could return to its cursed state."

Elowen's gaze was steady. "Then we keep going."

They followed the path, the flowers parting as they walked, their petals brushing against Elowen's fingers like whispers of encouragement. She felt the forest's magic, and for the first time, it was welcoming—warm, as if the land itself was guiding them.

The Grove of Ancients

The path led them to a massive grove, where trees stood taller and wider than any they had seen before. Their trunks were thick with age, their bark etched with runes that glowed faintly. In the center of the grove was a large stone circle, each stone covered in carvings that depicted fae figures, animals, and swirling vines. At the center of this circle stood an altar, made from the same dark stone as the surrounding pillars.

"This place is ancient," Elowen whispered, her eyes scanning the carvings. "Older than the Queen, older than the forest's curse."

Periwinkle's ears twitched as he walked toward the altar, his eyes gleaming with recognition. "These are the Forest Guardians," he said. "Spirits of the land that existed long before the Thistle Queen claimed her throne. They watched over this place, keeping its magic balanced."

Rook ran his fingers over one of the stones, tracing the carvings. "What happened to them?"

Periwinkle's eyes darkened. "When the Queen's curse took hold, their power was weakened. She used her magic to bind them, trapping their essence within the forest itself. But now that the curse is lifted, they may be free."

As he spoke, the air around them shimmered. The carvings on the stones began to glow brighter, and the runes shifted, rearranging themselves into new patterns. Light poured from the altar, and from the base of each stone, figures emerged—ethereal forms, tall and cloaked in robes made of leaves and petals. They were the Guardians, their eyes filled with ancient wisdom and sorrow.

Elowen, Rook, and Periwinkle stepped back as the Guardians moved, their voices a chorus that echoed through the grove.

"We are the ones who watch," they intoned. "We are the keepers of the forest's soul. You have broken the curse, but the balance remains fragile."

Elowen stepped forward, her heart pounding. "We seek to restore the forest's balance. Tell us what we must do."

The Guardians turned their gazes upon her, and she felt the weight of their presence, as if the entire forest were looking through their eyes. "The Queen was but one piece of the puzzle," they said. "Her power was tied to the forest, but it was not its origin."

Rook crossed his arms, his brow furrowed. "If she wasn't the source, then what is?"

The Guardians gestured toward the altar, and a symbol appeared—a circle surrounded by thorns, with a tree at its center. "The heart of the forest lies beyond the veil, in the place where the physical and the magical realms converge. It is the birthplace of Thrysseldown's magic, the origin of all that grows here."

Elowen's eyes narrowed. "And what lies in this heart?"

Periwinkle's voice was low. "The forest's spirit, and the source of its true power. When the Queen's curse took hold, it corrupted that spirit, binding it to her will. To truly free the forest, we must cleanse the heart and restore its original power."

The Guardians nodded. "But be warned. The heart is guarded by the remnants of the curse—creatures born of shadow and pain. You must face them and prove your worth."

Rook sighed, his hand resting on the hilt of his dagger. "Of course, it's never that simple."

The Veil Between Realms

The Guardians raised their hands, and the air around the altar shimmered, splitting like a curtain being drawn aside. A portal appeared, its edges glowing with silver light. Beyond it lay a swirling expanse of mist, thick and impenetrable.

"The veil between realms," Periwinkle said. "It's the gateway to the heart of the forest. Once we enter, we'll be in a place where the rules of the physical world don't apply. Magic will be stronger there, and so will the Queen's influence."

Elowen felt a chill, but her resolve was firm. "We've come this far. We can't turn back now."

Rook offered a grin, though his eyes held a hint of fear. "Into the unknown, then."

Together, they stepped through the portal. The air was cool and heavy, and as they crossed the threshold, the world around them shifted. The grove faded, replaced by a landscape of swirling mist and towering trees whose trunks seemed to stretch infinitely into the sky. The ground beneath them was soft, like moss, and it pulsed with energy.

They had entered the heart of Thrysseldown—a place where the magic of the forest was raw and untamed. The light was dim, filtered through the mist that clung to everything, and the air was thick with the scent of damp earth and flowers. Every step sent ripples through the ground, and Elowen could feel the forest's power, a hum that vibrated through her bones.

"Stay close," Periwinkle warned. "This place is alive. It will test us."

The Guardians of the Heart

As they ventured deeper into the mist, shadows began to move at the edges of their vision. Shapes formed and dissolved—some looked like animals, others like people, their faces obscured and their forms twisted. The air grew colder, and the ground beneath their feet felt unstable, as if they were walking on the surface of a shifting sea.

The shadows solidified into figures—creatures of darkness, their bodies made of thorns and bark, their eyes glowing with the same green fire as the Thistle Queen's. They were the remnants of the curse, the final guardians of the forest's heart.

"There," Periwinkle said, nodding toward a massive tree in the distance. Its trunk was twisted, its branches reaching out like claws. "The heart of Thrysseldown."

Elowen could see a faint light pulsing within the tree, like a heartbeat. But the creatures moved to block their path, their eyes fixed on the intruders. "We have to get past them," she said, readying her knife.

Rook nodded, his face set with determination. "Time to put an end to this."

The creatures attacked, their movements swift and silent. Elowen and Rook fought back, their weapons clashing against the creatures' thorny limbs. The shadows hissed as they struck, their forms shifting like smoke, but their claws were sharp, and every blow felt like a stab of ice.

Periwinkle darted between them, his movements quick and precise. He lunged at the creatures, his claws tearing through the darkness. "They're not like the others," he growled. "These are the forest's last defenses."

Elowen felt the strain as she battled the creatures. For every one they struck down, another seemed to rise in its place, the shadows reforming from the mist. The air was thick with the scent of magic, and the ground beneath their feet pulsed with each heartbeat from the tree.

"We need to reach the heart," she shouted, her voice carrying over the clash of battle. "If we can cleanse it, these creatures will fall."

Rook and Periwinkle nodded, and together, they pushed forward, cutting through the swarm of creatures. The light within the tree grew brighter, pulsing faster as they neared. Elowen could feel the magic building, a crescendo that hummed in the air.

The Cleansing Ritual

As they reached the base of the tree, the creatures pulled back, circling them like predators waiting for the right moment to strike. The bark of the tree was rough and cold, its surface covered in runes that pulsed with dark energy. The heart of the forest was close, but its corruption was palpable.

Elowen reached into her satchel, pulling out the last of her herbs and oils. "We have to perform a cleansing ritual," she said, spreading the mixture over the roots of the tree. "We need to purify the heart."

Periwinkle's eyes glowed as he began to chant, his voice merging with the energy of the forest. "Spirits of the forest, hear us. We seek to restore the balance, to bring light where darkness has taken hold."

Rook held off the creatures, his movements a blur as he fought with everything he had. "Hurry up!" he shouted, deflecting another attack. "They're getting stronger!"

Elowen pressed her hands to the tree, her voice joining Periwinkle's. She felt the magic surge through her, a connection to the forest that went deeper than anything she had felt before. The light within the tree responded, growing brighter, pushing back the darkness.

The creatures howled, their forms writhing as the magic of the cleansing ritual spread through the ground. The shadows twisted, their shapes breaking apart as the light intensified.

"Elowen, now!" Periwinkle urged.

Elowen focused all her energy, channeling the power of the herbs, the earth, and the magic within her. She felt the connection to the forest strengthen, and with one final surge, she sent the light coursing through the tree.

The air exploded with brightness, and the creatures dissolved into the mist, their screams fading into silence. The light enveloped the tree, and the runes glowed with a brilliant white, washing away the darkness.

When the light faded, the forest was still. The tree's twisted form had smoothed, its bark glowing softly, and the air was filled with the scent of flowers and fresh rain.

The heart of Thrysseldown was cleansed.

Elowen, Rook, and Periwinkle stood before the tree, their breaths heavy but their hearts light. The forest's balance had been restored, and its magic, once dark and twisted, was now pure and vibrant.

But as they looked into the tree's light, a figure emerged—a spirit of the forest, its form graceful and ethereal. It bowed to them, its eyes filled with gratitude. "You have saved the heart of Thrysseldown. The forest is yours to protect."

Elowen felt the weight of those words. The curse had been lifted, but the responsibility now fell to them. Together, they would guide the forest into a new age, one where light and life could flourish once more.

But their journey was far from over. The forest held many secrets, and the road ahead would be long.

The Spirit of the Forest

As the figure emerged from the heart of the tree, it seemed to glide, its form shimmering like the surface of a lake under moonlight. The Spirit of Thrysseldown was both human and not—its body was woven from leaves, flowers, and the glow of ancient magic. Its eyes were deep green, like the forest's depths, and they held centuries of knowledge, sorrow, and hope.

Elowen, Rook, and Periwinkle watched, still catching their breath, as the spirit approached. Elowen felt a mixture of awe and trepidation; the spirit was beautiful, but its presence radiated an immense power that made her feel small, like a single leaf in the vast canopy of the forest.

The Spirit inclined its head, and when it spoke, its voice was a soft, echoing whisper, like the wind through the leaves. "You have undone the curse and cleansed the heart of Thrysseldown. For this, you have my gratitude."

Elowen stepped forward, her eyes meeting the spirit's. "We did what was necessary. But there is still much I don't understand. How did the curse begin? And why was the Thistle Queen bound to it?"

The Spirit's gaze shifted, as if peering into a distant past. "The curse was born from a betrayal long forgotten. The Thistle Queen, Nyssara, was once the guardian of this forest, its protector and its heart. But she fell in love with a mortal—a love that defied the natural laws of our realm. In her desperation to save him, she used the forest's power to bind his soul, corrupting the balance and intertwining her fate with his."

Rook, leaning on his dagger, shook his head. "So, the curse wasn't just about power—it was about love."

Periwinkle, standing at Elowen's side, added, "And that love, tainted by desperation and sorrow, became a curse that bound not just Nyssara, but the forest itself."

The Spirit nodded. "The Queen's sorrow and regret twisted the forest's magic. The spirits that once guarded this place became imprisoned within its shadows, and the balance was lost. The forest, once a realm of life and light, was transformed into a place of darkness and thorns."

Elowen felt a pang of sympathy for the Thistle Queen. "She was trapped by her own choices."

The Spirit's eyes softened. "Yes, and in freeing her, you have restored part of that balance. But the forest's magic is ancient and deep, and the effects of the curse linger still. To fully heal Thrysseldown, you must unlock the secrets that were hidden when the curse took hold."

Elowen exchanged a glance with Rook and Periwinkle. "How do we do that?"

The Spirit gestured to the glowing runes on the tree's bark. "There are three artifacts—keys that once maintained the harmony between the forest and its guardian. When Nyssara's curse fractured that harmony, these artifacts were hidden, scattered across the forest's realms to prevent them from being used against her."

Rook let out a sigh. "Of course. Nothing's ever straightforward."

Periwinkle's eyes narrowed. "What are these artifacts?"

The Spirit's form wavered, and the images of the artifacts appeared in the air—three ethereal shapes floating like ghostly silhouettes. The first was a small vial, its contents glowing a brilliant blue, as if filled with the essence of moonlight. The second was a pendant shaped like a crescent moon, its surface etched with runes that pulsed with magic. The third was a staff made of twisted wood, its tip adorned with a crystal that shone with a green light, mirroring the eyes of the spirit itself.

"These are the Forest Keys," the Spirit explained. "The Vial of Echoes, the Moonstone Pendant, and the Verdant Staff. Each holds a part of the forest's power and memory. To restore the balance, you must find them, unlock their magic, and return them to the heart of the forest."

Elowen stared at the images, committing each detail to memory. "Where are they?"

The Spirit's expression turned somber. "They lie within the three domains of the forest that remain corrupted. You have restored the heart, but these areas are still under the influence of the curse's remnants. Only by purifying these places and retrieving the artifacts can you truly heal Thrysseldown."

Rook's eyes flicked to the spirit. "And I'm guessing these places won't just let us walk in and take what we need?"

Periwinkle's ears twitched, his eyes serious. "No, they won't. The curse's magic will fight back, and the guardians of each domain—creatures born of shadow and pain—will test us."

The Three Domains

The Spirit raised its hand, and the grove shifted, showing glimpses of each of the three domains. The first was a marshland, shrouded in mist and filled with dark waters where twisted roots emerged like grasping hands. The second was a glade where moonlight shone perpetually, illuminating a circle of stone pillars covered in vines and flowers that bloomed in the dark. The third was a mountain shrouded in dense fog, its summit hidden by swirling clouds, and at its base lay a grove where the trees grew in unnatural patterns, their trunks twisted into eerie shapes.

"These are the domains you must enter," the Spirit continued. "The Marsh of Shadows, the Glade of Echoes, and the Misty Peak. Each contains an artifact, but they are protected by powerful magic. Only with courage, unity, and the knowledge you have gained will you be able to overcome the trials that await."

Elowen felt the weight of the task settle on her shoulders. "We'll do it. We have to."

Rook nodded, though a hint of worry lingered in his eyes. "Well, I suppose we've faced worse. But these places look like they were designed to kill."

Periwinkle's eyes glowed with determination. "We have no choice. The forest's survival—and our own—depends on it."

The Spirit's form began to fade, its light dimming as the energy that had held it together waned. "I have given you what guidance I can. The rest is up to you. Remember, the forest's magic responds to both light and darkness. It will amplify your fears, but it will also amplify your courage. Trust in each other, and you may find the strength you need."

Elowen watched as the Spirit dissolved into the air, leaving them alone in the grove. The air felt heavier now, charged with purpose and the gravity of their mission. She turned to her companions, her eyes full of determination. "We have to move quickly. If these domains are still corrupted, we need to purify them before the forest is overrun again."

Periwinkle nodded. "The Marsh of Shadows is closest. We'll start there."

The Marsh of Shadows

The journey to the marsh was eerie, the mist growing thicker as they moved deeper into the forest. The air became humid, and the ground beneath their feet grew softer, turning into mud that clung to their boots. The trees in this part of the forest were gnarled and twisted, their branches hanging low like skeletal fingers. The atmosphere was heavy, and the silence was broken only by the occasional croak of a distant frog or the splash of something unseen moving through the dark waters.

Elowen felt the familiar tingle of magic prickling at her senses. "We're getting close. I can feel the energy shifting."

Rook, his eyes scanning the murky landscape, muttered, "Feels like something's watching us."

Periwinkle's fur bristled. "The marsh is home to the Wraithroot—a creature born of the Queen's magic. It guards the Vial of Echoes, and it feeds on fear."

Elowen's eyes narrowed. "What is it, exactly?"

Periwinkle's voice was grave. "A spirit that lurks in the water and shadows. It can appear as a lost soul, a friendly face, or a nightmare—anything that makes you hesitate. It draws its victims into the marsh, and once you're caught, you become part of its domain."

Rook gripped his dagger tighter. "So, don't trust what we see. Got it."

As they moved deeper into the marsh, the fog thickened, obscuring their vision. The ground beneath their feet turned to shallow water, and twisted roots emerged from the muck like claws. The air was filled with a damp chill, and every splash or rustle made them jump.

Ahead, a faint light flickered—a soft blue glow, like the one they had seen in the vision of the vial. "That's it," Elowen whispered. "The Vial of Echoes."

But as they approached, the light flickered, and the water around them rippled. The shadows stretched, and figures began to emerge from the mist—ghostly shapes that looked like people, their faces pale and eyes blank.

"Elowen," one of the figures whispered, stepping closer. It was the form of a young woman, her hair long and dark, her eyes wide with fear. "You left me. Why didn't you come back?"

Elowen's breath caught in her throat. It was her sister—an image she hadn't seen in years, not since she had left her family behind to work at the castle. "No," she whispered. "This isn't real."

The figure's face twisted into a sneer. "You abandoned me. You cared more about plants than your own family."

Elowen felt a surge of guilt, but Periwinkle's voice cut through the fog. "It's the Wraithroot—ignore it. It's trying to weaken you."

Rook faced his own vision—a shadowy figure of his mother, her face full of disappointment. "You've always been a failure, Rook. You'll never be more than a thief."

Rook's hand shook, but he clenched his teeth. "I know what you are," he muttered, stepping back from the figure. "And you're not her."

The shadows hissed, their forms becoming monstrous, their eyes turning a sickly green. The Wraithroot emerged from the water, its body a mass of tendrils and shadowy vines, its face constantly shifting between those of their loved ones. "You cannot escape your fears," it hissed, its voice echoing in their minds.

Elowen tightened her grip on her knife. "We're not here to escape. We're here to end this."

She reached for the pouch at her side, pulling out a mixture of herbs infused with the same oil she'd used at the heart of the forest. With a quick motion, she spread it over the blade of her knife. "Rook, Periwinkle—distract it. I need to get close."

Rook nodded, and Periwinkle leapt forward, his fox form blurring as he dodged the Wraithroot's tendrils. The creature lashed out, but its attacks were clumsy, driven by its need to intimidate rather than strike. Rook slashed at the vines, giving Elowen the opening she needed.

With a swift movement, she plunged her knife into the heart of the Wraithroot. The creature screamed, its form writhing as the magic from the herbs spread through its body. The blue light of the Vial of Echoes flared, illuminating the marsh as the shadows dissolved into mist.

The Wraithroot's body disintegrated, and the vial floated in the air, its glow pure and bright. Elowen reached out, taking it in her hands. The moment she touched it, she felt the power within—a connection to the forest's past, a memory waiting to be unlocked.

"One down," she said, her voice steady but tired. "Two more to go."

The marsh slowly cleared, and the path beyond opened. The forest had given them their first victory, but the true challenge still lay ahead, waiting in the moonlit glade and the misty peak.

The Glade of Echoes

With the Vial of Echoes secured, the trio left the marsh behind. The air cleared as they moved forward, and the forest's landscape shifted, becoming less tangled and more open. The trees grew taller, their branches reaching gracefully overhead, and the path before them widened into a soft, grassy trail. The mist lifted, revealing a soft glow in the distance—the moonlit expanse of the Glade of Echoes.

As they neared, the moonlight intensified, and Elowen felt a shiver run down her spine. The path led to an open glade surrounded by stone pillars, each one covered in blooming vines and delicate flowers that seemed to thrive under the perpetual moonlight. The air was cooler here, and the scent of night-blooming jasmine filled the air. The glade seemed peaceful, almost serene, but Elowen knew better. There was an energy, an ancient tension that lingered like a whispered warning.

"The Glade of Echoes," Periwinkle said, his voice barely above a whisper. "It's a place where the forest's memory is strongest. It's where the Moonstone Pendant is hidden."

Rook glanced around, his eyes wary. "Doesn't seem too dangerous. Almost... peaceful."

Periwinkle's fur bristled as he scanned the glade. "The peace is a facade. The glade reflects the emotions of those who enter. It draws from your heart, your thoughts, and it manifests what lies beneath. Be cautious."

Elowen nodded, feeling the weight of his warning. "We need to stay together. No matter what we see, we can't let it separate us."

Entering the Glade

The trio stepped into the glade, and the air felt different—lighter, almost as if they were crossing into another realm. The moonlight above shone brighter, casting long shadows that stretched across the grass. The pillars surrounding the glade seemed to hum, their runes glowing softly. As they moved further in, the temperature dropped, and the light of the moon seemed to focus on the center of the glade where a raised stone altar stood.

On the altar, they saw it: the Moonstone Pendant, glowing with a silvery light. Its surface shimmered as if it held the moon's reflection, and the runes etched into it pulsed with the rhythm of the forest's magic.

"There it is," Elowen said, her eyes locked on the pendant. "We have to be careful."

Rook nodded, his gaze fixed on the pendant. "No sudden moves."

As they advanced, the air grew colder, and a soft whisper echoed through the glade. The sound was gentle at first, like the rustle of leaves, but it grew louder, turning into overlapping voices that surrounded them. The whispers became clearer, words emerging that tugged at their hearts.

"Elowen... come home..."

"Elowen, you were always meant to be alone..."

"Elowen, why did you leave?"

Elowen froze. She recognized the voices—her family, the people she had left behind to pursue her own path. She felt a pang of guilt, the familiar ache she had pushed down for years.

The air around her grew thick, and her vision blurred as the glade transformed.

Suddenly, she wasn't standing in the glade anymore. She was back in the garden of her childhood home. The flowers she and her mother had planted together bloomed all around her, and she saw her younger self running through the rows of plants. Her mother's voice called out, and she saw her, standing by the gate, smiling.

"Elowen, you were supposed to stay," the vision of her mother said, her voice soft but tinged with sadness. "The garden is dying without you."

Elowen felt tears prick at her eyes, but she forced herself to stay focused. "This isn't real," she whispered. "It's the glade trying to trap me."

She reached for the pendant, her hand outstretched, but the vision of her mother blocked her path, her face twisting into an expression of sorrow. "You left, Elowen. And you'll leave them too. You'll always choose the forest over those you love."

Elowen hesitated, her hand trembling. She could feel the truth of the words digging into her heart. But then she heard Periwinkle's voice, distant but strong. "Elowen, focus! It's a lie!"

The words pierced through the illusion, and Elowen blinked. The garden around her wavered, the flowers wilting and turning to shadow. She clenched her jaw, pushing past the vision. "I won't be held back by the past," she said, her voice resolute.

The illusion shattered, and she found herself back in the glade, her hand inches from the pendant. She grabbed it, feeling its cool surface pulse with magic. The whispers faded, and the moonlight dimmed, revealing the true, silent glade.

Rook's Trial: The Lost Path

But while Elowen had broken free of the glade's influence, Rook was not so fortunate. He stood motionless a few feet away, his eyes distant and unfocused. The glade had ensnared him, drawing him into a vision of his own making.

Rook saw himself standing before a path that split into two. On one side was the city he had grown up in, filled with familiar faces—people he had stolen from, lied to, and betrayed. On the other side was a dark, lonely road, shrouded in mist. It was the road he had taken when he chose to abandon everything, to run and live as a thief.

As he stood there, the faces of the people he had wronged appeared, their eyes accusing. "You only know how to run," they said, their voices cold. "You'll never be more than a coward."

He felt the weight of their words, the shame creeping up like a shadow. But then he heard another voice—softer, and yet somehow more powerful. It was Elowen's. "Rook, you've already faced this. You're not running now. Don't let it pull you in."

Rook blinked, the vision wavering. He looked down the lonely road again, but this time, he saw something different. He saw Elowen and Periwinkle standing with him, their faces determined. He realized that he wasn't alone anymore, that he had chosen to stay and fight.

With a deep breath, he stepped forward, shattering the vision. The glade dissolved, and he found himself back beside Elowen, the pendant glowing between them. "Guess I almost fell for that one," he said with a grin, though there was a tremor in his voice.

Elowen offered him a reassuring smile. "But you didn't. We're stronger together."

The Moonstone's Power

Periwinkle watched as they reunited, his eyes reflecting the pendant's glow. "The Moonstone Pendant is one of the keys, but it's also a beacon. It holds the memory of the forest's magic—the connection between the fae and the mortal world. It will guide us to the Misty Peak."

Elowen lifted the pendant, feeling its weight. The moment her fingers closed around it, she felt a rush of memories—not her own, but the forest's. She saw glimpses of its past—fae dancing in the moonlight, the forest flourishing under their care, and then the moment when everything twisted, the trees turning dark and the flowers wilting as the curse took hold.

She saw Nyssara, the Thistle Queen, standing alone, her eyes filled with pain as the curse consumed her. "This is the forest's history," Elowen murmured, her voice distant. "It's showing us what was lost."

Rook looked up at the moon, his face somber. "And what we have to restore."

The pendant's glow intensified, and the light formed a path leading out of the glade, toward the looming silhouette of the mountain shrouded in mist. "The Misty Peak is the last domain," Periwinkle said. "It's where the Verdant Staff lies—the final key to restoring the forest's balance."

Elowen nodded, her eyes burning with determination. "Let's go."

The Misty Peak

The path wound through the forest, leading them to the base of the Misty Peak. The mountain loomed overhead, its summit hidden by swirling clouds and dense fog. The air grew colder as they climbed, and the mist thickened, obscuring their vision. The scent of pine and earth filled the air, and the ground beneath their feet was rough, covered in roots and loose stones.

As they ascended, the fog grew thicker, turning into a swirling veil that clung to their skin and clothes. Elowen's breath formed clouds in the chill, and she could barely see a few feet in front of her. "Stay close," she called, her voice muffled by the fog.

Periwinkle's eyes glowed as he led the way, his form a shadowy silhouette against the mist. "The peak is a place of illusions," he warned. "The fog will show us our fears, our desires—anything to lead us astray."

Rook shivered, his hand resting on the hilt of his dagger. "This place gives me the creeps."

As they climbed, the fog thickened, and Elowen felt the air grow heavy. The path split into multiple trails, each disappearing into the dense fog. The pendant in her hand glowed faintly, its light barely penetrating the mist.

Suddenly, the fog shifted, and a shape emerged—a towering figure made of twisted roots and brambles, its eyes burning with green fire. It stood at the center of the path, blocking their way. "Turn back," it growled, its voice rumbling like thunder. "The peak is not for the living."

Elowen felt the magic surge through the air, and she gripped the pendant tightly. "We're not leaving. We've come for the Verdant Staff."

The guardian's eyes flared, and the fog around them twisted, forming shadowy figures that surrounded the trio. The air hummed with magic, and the ground trembled as the figures advanced.

"Prepare yourselves," Periwinkle said, his voice low. "This is the final test."

The Guardian's Test

The shadowy figures lunged, their forms shifting between human and beast, their claws slashing through the mist. Elowen dodged the first attack, her knife flashing as she struck back. Rook moved beside her, his movements quick and precise as he defended against the shadows. Periwinkle leapt through the fog, his fox form a blur of motion.

The guardian roared, and the roots beneath their feet surged, wrapping around their legs. Elowen felt the pull of the earth, the weight of the mountain's power bearing down on her. "Rook, Periwinkle—we have to break its connection to the mountain!"

Periwinkle's eyes flashed. "Aim for the roots! It's drawing power from the earth."

Rook slashed at the roots, his dagger cutting through the vines. "On it!"

Elowen raised the pendant, its light intensifying as she focused her energy. She felt the forest's magic, the connection between the pendant and the mountain's peak. "By the light of the moon, by the heart of the forest, I command you—release your hold!"

The pendant's light exploded, washing over the guardian and the fog. The roots recoiled, and the shadowy figures dissolved into mist. The guardian's eyes dimmed, its form collapsing into a pile of twisted roots and earth.

As the fog cleared, the path to the peak opened, revealing a small grove where the Verdant Staff stood, its crystal glowing with a bright green light. Elowen, Rook, and Periwinkle approached, their breaths heavy but their spirits triumphant.

Elowen reached for the staff, and the moment her fingers touched the wood, she felt the forest's power surge through her. The final key was theirs.

The three artifacts—the Vial of Echoes, the Moonstone Pendant, and the Verdant Staff—glowed together, their lights merging as the forest's magic united.

"We've done it," Rook said, a grin spreading across his face. "Now, let's finish this."

Elowen raised the staff, its light illuminating the mountain peak. "It's time to restore Thrysseldown."

The path back to the heart of the forest lay before them, and with the three keys in hand, they were ready to face the final challenge—the true source of the forest's curse.

The Final Ascent

With the three keys—the Vial of Echoes, the Moonstone Pendant, and the Verdant Staff—glowing in their hands, Elowen, Rook, and Periwinkle began their descent from the Misty Peak. The fog that had once obscured their path now parted before them, and the air felt charged with anticipation. The forest itself seemed to respond to the presence of the artifacts, the trees whispering softly as if urging them forward.

The trio retraced their steps, moving swiftly through the transformed forest. The path wound between towering trees, their branches arching overhead, and the ground was soft with moss that pulsed with a faint, magical light. As they walked, Elowen could feel the power of the artifacts resonating with the forest, each step drawing them closer to the heart where the final confrontation awaited.

"The forest knows we're coming," Periwinkle said, his voice low. "It's shifting in response to the keys. The magic is aligning itself."

Rook tightened his grip on the hilt of his dagger. "And the Thistle Queen's magic? Will she be waiting for us?"

Elowen's eyes were steady. "Her spirit is gone, but the curse's remnants linger. Whatever remains of her power will fight to hold onto the forest. We have to be prepared for anything."

Periwinkle nodded. "The heart of Thrysseldown was cleansed, but the corruption is deep. The artifacts must be returned to their rightful place to fully restore the balance."

As they approached the grove where the altar stood, the air grew heavier, and a familiar coldness settled over the forest. The path, which had been wide and open, narrowed, the trees pressing closer as if trying to block their way. Shadows danced at the edges of their vision, and the whispers that once guided them now twisted into eerie echoes, distorted and hostile.

The Ruptured Grove

The trio stepped into the grove that held the stone altar, but it was no longer the serene place they had seen before. The ground was fractured, and dark vines snaked their way up the ancient stones, wrapping around the pillars like chains. The light from the altar, once pure, now flickered like a dying flame. The forest's energy felt strained, as if it were struggling against an unseen force.

Elowen's heart sank. "The curse is fighting back."

As they moved closer, the shadows solidified into figures—twisted and grotesque forms of the fae, their faces a mask of pain and anger. They were the remnants of those who had once guarded the forest, now corrupted and enslaved by the curse's power.

"We have to free them," Elowen said, her voice filled with determination. "They're part of the forest's balance."

The figures advanced, their eyes glowing with a sickly green light. Their movements were slow but deliberate, and as they closed in, the air grew colder, and the light from the altar dimmed further.

Rook raised his dagger, ready to defend. "I'm guessing they won't just let us pass."

Periwinkle's eyes narrowed. "They are bound to the curse. We need to break their connection before they overwhelm us."

Elowen lifted the Moonstone Pendant, its light flaring in response to her touch. She held it high, and the runes on its surface pulsed, casting a silvery glow over the grove. "We can't fight them with weapons alone," she said. "The pendant holds the memory of the forest's magic—we have to remind them who they were."

She stepped forward, the light from the pendant enveloping one of the figures. Its form wavered, the shadow peeling away to reveal a glimpse of its original self—a fae with eyes like golden leaves and skin that glowed faintly.

The figure hesitated, its eyes meeting Elowen's. "I... remember," it whispered, its voice a mournful echo. "The forest... the dance of the seasons..."

As the pendant's light washed over it, the shadow fully dissolved, leaving behind the fae's true form. It bowed its head in gratitude before fading into the light, its spirit freed.

Rook and Periwinkle joined Elowen, holding off the remaining figures as she continued to use the pendant's magic. One by one, the shadows wavered, their forms flickering as the light purified them, transforming them back into their original state.

With each figure she freed, the grove brightened, and the vines that had ensnared the stones began to retreat. The air felt lighter, and the whispers shifted, becoming softer and more harmonious.

Reclaiming the Heart

As the last of the corrupted fae was restored, the grove transformed. The altar, once dim and overgrown, now shone with a vibrant green light. The trees around them swayed, their leaves shimmering as the forest's magic resonated with the presence of the artifacts.

Elowen approached the altar, the Vial of Echoes and the Verdant Staff in her hands. "This is where the artifacts belong," she said. "Together, they will restore the heart's power."

Rook and Periwinkle stood beside her as she placed the Vial of Echoes on the altar. Its blue light flared, illuminating the runes etched into the stone. The air around them shimmered, and the whispering trees seemed to sing, their voices intertwining with the hum of magic.

Next, she raised the Verdant Staff. The moment its crystal touched the altar, a pulse of energy surged through the grove, spreading out like ripples in a pond. The runes glowed with an intense green light, and the ground beneath them trembled as the forest's power awakened.

The Moonstone Pendant glowed brightly, and Elowen held it above the altar. As its light merged with the other two artifacts, the grove's energy intensified. The pillars surrounding the altar thrummed with power, their runes shifting and aligning as the magic of the forest coalesced.

A burst of light erupted from the altar, shooting up into the canopy above. The light spread, weaving through the trees, and as it moved, the darkness that had plagued the forest began to lift. The vines that had choked the life from the trees recoiled, turning to dust, and the flowers that had been blackened and twisted bloomed once more, their petals vibrant and full of life.

The Forest Awakes

The forest transformed before their eyes. The once-darkened trees glowed with a soft, golden light, and the ground beneath them erupted with flowers in every shade—bluebells, nightshade blooms, and moonflowers. The air was filled with the scent of earth and rain, a promise of renewal.

Elowen, Rook, and Periwinkle watched as the magic of the forest awakened fully. The grove, now vibrant and alive, pulsed with the energy of the reunited artifacts. The whispers in the air became a song—a hymn of gratitude and peace.

As the light dimmed to a gentle glow, the Spirit of the Forest appeared once more. Its form was stronger now, fully realized and woven from the essence of the land itself. It smiled, its eyes reflecting the gratitude of the entire forest.

"You have done what no others could," the Spirit said. "The balance of Thrysseldown has been restored, and the curse that plagued this land has been lifted. The forest will thrive once more."

Elowen felt a wave of relief wash over her. "We didn't do it alone," she said. "The forest guided us."

The Spirit nodded. "And you listened. You have become the new guardians of this land, the stewards of its magic. With the artifacts restored, the forest's power will flow freely once again, but it requires those who will protect and nurture it."

Rook rubbed the back of his neck, a grin spreading across his face. "Guardians, huh? Never thought I'd be a hero."

Periwinkle's eyes shone with pride. "You've earned it."

The Promise of a New Age

Elowen felt the weight of the pendant in her hand, its light a steady pulse that mirrored her own heartbeat. "The artifacts belong here, but what happens now?"

The Spirit gestured to the grove, where the altar and the pillars still pulsed with the forest's magic. "You will rebuild. The fae and the mortals will walk this land together again, and the forest will become what it once was—a place of balance, beauty, and life."

Rook stepped forward, his expression serious. "And the Queen? Will she ever return?"

The Spirit's eyes softened. "Nyssara's spirit has moved on, but her influence will remain. Her legacy is tied to this land, and her memory will serve as a reminder of what can happen when power is misused. But as long as you protect this place, her darkness will never take hold again."

Periwinkle's form shimmered, and for a moment, his true fae form was visible—a regal figure with golden eyes and a crown of leaves. "We will protect it," he vowed. "This forest is our home, and we will ensure its magic remains pure."

Elowen raised the staff, and the light from the pendant and vial joined with its glow, casting a radiant warmth over the grove. The forest's energy thrummed through her, and she felt the strength and life of the land flow into her. "We will rebuild, together."

The forest's magic pulsed in response, and the trees swayed as if nodding in agreement. The vines bloomed, the flowers opened, and the light of the moon shone down, bathing the grove in a silver glow.

Epilogue: A Forest Renewed

Months passed, and the forest flourished. The paths that had once been choked with thorns now bloomed with flowers and lush greenery. Elowen, Rook, and Periwinkle worked tirelessly, guiding the fae and mortals who returned to the forest to restore its beauty and magic. The grove became a sanctuary, the heart of Thrysseldown's power.

Elowen felt at home among the trees, her connection to the land stronger than ever. Rook, no longer a thief but a protector, helped guide travelers who came to seek the forest's wisdom. Periwinkle remained their guardian, his knowledge and magic ensuring the balance was upheld.

As the forest thrived, it became a place where light and shadow coexisted in harmony, a testament to the power of unity and trust. And in the center of the grove, where the three artifacts lay, the heart of the forest pulsed—a reminder that even the darkest curses could be broken when courage, love, and hope worked together.

The forest of Thrysseldown was reborn, and its song, once a whisper, became a chorus of life, echoing through the ages.

Don't miss out!

Visit the website below and you can sign up to receive emails whenever Catherine J Rosser publishes a new book. There's no charge and no obligation.

https://books2read.com/r/B-A-FGQOC-IEZCF

BOOKS 2 READ

Connecting independent readers to independent writers.

Did you love *The Thistle Queen*? Then you should read *The Magic Within*[1] by Catherine J Rosser!

The Eternal Magic Series: Book One – *The Magic Within*

Aelia has always felt different, a power simmering beneath her skin that she neither understands nor controls. When this mysterious magic awakens, it forces her to flee the only life she's known to protect her family. Lost and fearful of the power that courses through her, Aelia embarks on a journey of self-discovery, uncovering the hidden legacy of her bloodline.

But Aelia's magic isn't just a gift—it's a responsibility. Tied to the flow of time itself, her power allows her to age slowly,

---

1. https://books2read.com/u/4AMN2K

2. https://books2read.com/u/4AMN2K

keeping her unchanged while the world around her moves forward. As she struggles to accept this truth, a darker force emerges: the Shadowborne, a secretive and ruthless group hunting those with magic like hers. They will stop at nothing to control or destroy the ancient power she now wields.

Guided by a deep connection to the magic within her and a newfound ally, Kaelen, Aelia must navigate a world where magic is both revered and feared. Along the way, she learns that her family has been hidden and protected, but at a cost—memories of her are slowly fading from their minds. Saddened but resolute, Aelia leaves them in peace, knowing that their safety comes first.

Now, with the Shadowborne closing in and her family protected, Aelia must embrace her power, learn to master the magic she once feared, and prepare for the battle ahead. Her journey has only just begun.

The Magic Within is the first thrilling installment of **The Eternal Magic Series**, an epic tale of magic, immortality, and destiny. Aelia's path will lead her through centuries, but first, she must confront the power within and the enemies who seek to control it.

Read more at https://catherinejrosser.com/.

Also by Catherine J Rosser

The Eternal Magic Series
The Magic Within

Standalone
Beyond the Horizon
Echoes in the Abyss
Haven Falls
The Fractured Mind
The Next Chapter: Embracing Midlife with Purpose, Peace,
and Possibility
The Thistle Queen

Watch for more at https://catherinejrosser.com/.

About the Author

Catherine J. Rosser is a fantasy author who weaves together myth, magic, and unforgettable journeys. Known for her vivid storytelling and rich characters, she brings epic worlds to life with themes of destiny and self-discovery. When not writing, Catherine draws inspiration from nature, channeling its beauty into her imaginative tales.

Read more at https://catherinejrosser.com/.